Turner Publishing, Inc., wishes to thank all of the people who helped make this
book possible: William Hanna and Joseph Barbera, Roger Mayer, Jack Petrik, Cathy
Manolis, Woolsey Ackerman, Mary Beth Verhunce, and Film Roman.

Published by Turner Publishing, Inc.
A Subsidiary of Turner Broadcasting System, Inc.
One CNN Center, Box 105366
Atlanta, Georgia 30348-5366

"Friends to the End," "Money is Such a Beautiful Word," and "I Miss You" by Henry
Mancini and Leslie Bricusse. Music and lyrics © 1992 Turner Music Publishing, Inc.,
and RET Music, Inc. All rights reserved.

Tom and Jerry • Friends to the End
Adaptation by Wendy Wax.
Based on the screenplay by Dennis Marks.

Produced by Welcome Enterprises, Inc.
164 East 95th Street
New York, New York 10128

Project Director: Hiro Clark
Editor: Ellen Mendlow
Designer: Mary Tiegreen
Associate Designer: Dianna Russo

Distributed by Andrews and McMeel
A Universal Press Syndicate Company
4900 Main Street
Kansas City, Missouri 64112

ISBN: 1-878685-26-0

Library of Congress catalogue card number: 93-060040

Printed and bound in the United States by Ringier America,
New Berlin, Wisconsin.
10 9 8 7 6 5 4 3 2 1

TOM and JERRY™
FRIENDS TO THE END

Adaptation by Wendy Wax

To save the life of a young girl, this cat and mouse will have to do the impossible. They'll have to get along.

Turner Publishing, Inc.

ATLANTA

"Tom! Wake up, my darling kitty cat!"

Tom yawned and stretched. He'd been dreaming about a scrumptious feast—with that wimpy, pip-squeak mouse, Jerry, as dessert! Licking his lips, he dozed off....

"Oh, Thomas, dear! Hurry, hurry! It's moving day and we're leaving!" Tom awoke with a start. Moving day!?!

VROOM! VROOM! roared the family van in front of the house.

Tom dashed toward the front door, but when he passed Jerry's mouse hole, he stopped. Creeping up to the tiny door, he heard faint snores. Perfect, he thought with an evil grin. That lazy, no-good mouse would be left behind. But just to be sure, he nailed two boards across the mouse hole.

VRRRooooom!

Tom was out the door in a split second.

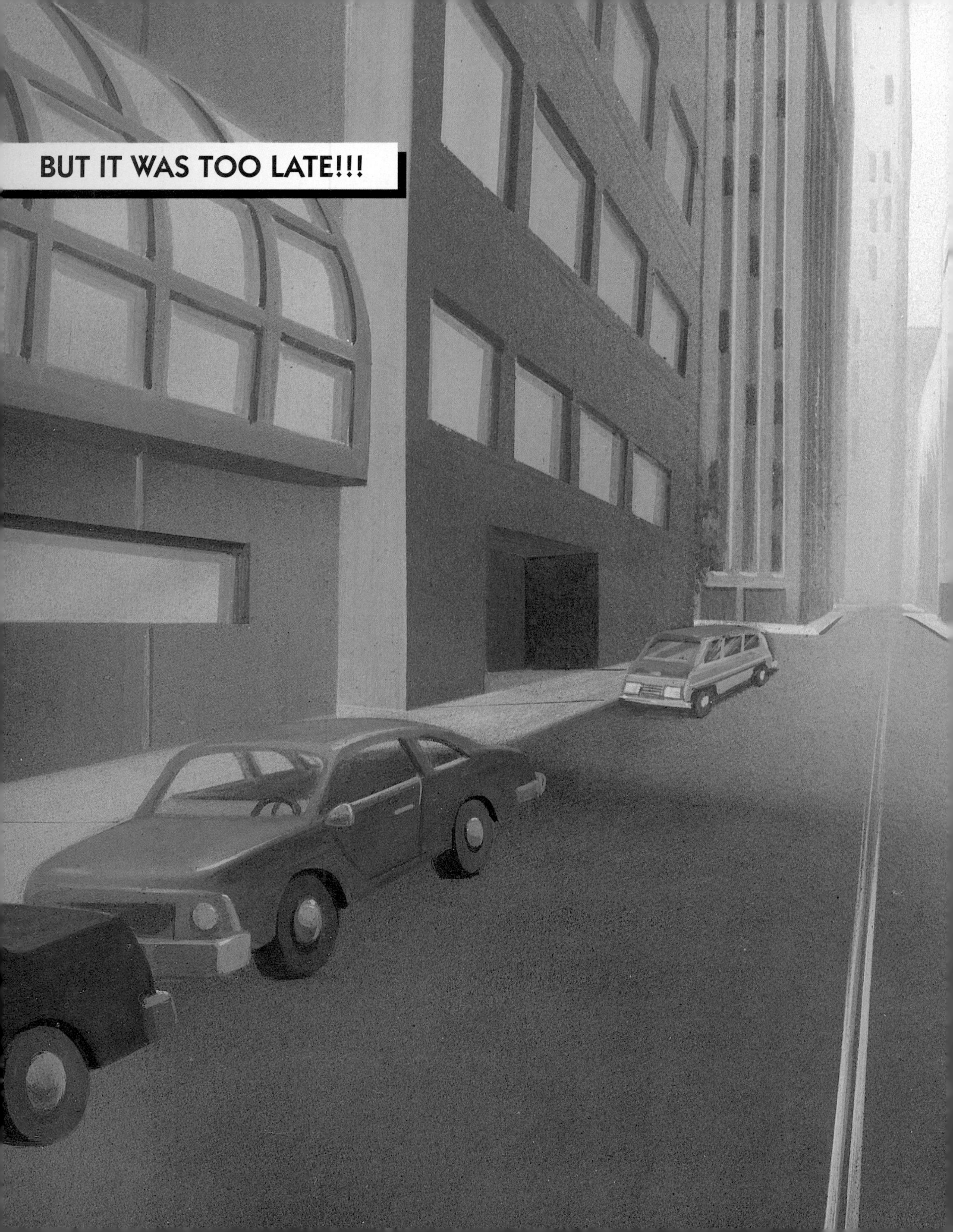
BUT IT WAS TOO LATE!!!

THE VAN WAS GONE.

Tom dragged himself sadly back into the house. It sure would be lonely with no family around. Who'd feed him and scratch his belly? He opened the door and **CRASH!** a gigantic wrecking ball swung through the front of the house, missing Tom by an inch! **BAM!** It went right through the rear wall and then back through the house again.

Startled out of his wits, Tom rushed outside—but then he remembered that pesky Jerry was still inside.

Meanwhile, Jerry also heard—and felt—the house shake. Was it an earthquake? Plaster fell from the ceiling, and his jars of cheese bits shat-

tered. He tried to scurry out the door, but he was locked in! Why, it had to be that horrible cat, Tom!

As much as Tom didn't like Jerry, he couldn't abandon him to the wrecking ball. He ran back into the house, ripped off the boards blocking the mouse hole, snatched Jerry up, and **WHAMMM!** The wrecking ball swung through again—this time destroying the house completely. But by now, Tom and Jerry were safe outside.

Tom set Jerry down and headed slowly down the street. Where could he go now?

PIT-PAT. PIT-PAT.

Tom stopped, turned around, and pointed the no-good pip-squeak in the other direction. But that didn't stop Jerry from following him. Tom climbed a fence. Jerry squeezed under it. Tom stopped in an alley, and— oops! Jerry ran right into him. Furiously, Tom grabbed Jerry by the tail and—

VAMOOSE, MOUSE!

"Well, well, well!" said a raspy voice. "Look at the big, brave pussycat pickin' on a poor little teensy-weensy mousie!" A scrappy-looking dog appeared from the shadows.

"Instead of bein' pals, you're fightin' like cat and mouse," said another voice. "Hey, you *are* a cat and mouse."

Tom and Jerry looked at each other and shrugged. Who said that? they wondered.

Suddenly a tiny speck did a flip on the dog's nose.

"Frankie Da Flea is the name."

"And I'm Puggsy," announced the dog.

"I'm Tom."

"And I'm Jerry."

The cat and the mouse turned to
each other in surprise.

"YOU TALKED!" they exclaimed
together. Neither one of them had ever
said a word to each other in all the
years they'd lived in the same house.

"Sure I talk," said Tom. "Whadda
ya think, I'm a dummy?"

"You said it, I didn't." Jerry giggled.

"That does it." Tom tried to
grab Jerry.

"Uh-uh-uh." Puggsy seized
Tom's wrist. "You guys gotta learn
to be friends."

"Ab-sotive-a-lutely!" Frankie
hopped onto Puggsy's hat. With
that, the two old pals began to sing:

12

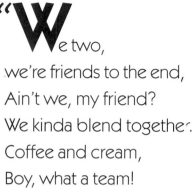e two,
we're friends to the end,
Ain't we, my friend?
We kinda blend together.
Coffee and cream,
Boy, what a team!

You'll never find two other guys,
Compatible as steak and fries!

We're two of a kind,
Much of a mind.
We find our way together
Thinking as one,
Searchin' for sunny skies!

True, the sun may turn to rain,
We don't mind a drop o' rain.
But you won't hear us complain!
Doesn't help to stop the rain.
What's to gain if we complain?
Causes lotsa stress an' strain.

We keep smilin' in the pitter-patter,
Doesn't matter!
Why let it drive us insane?

We know the weather will mend,
Won't it, my friend?
We'll weather life together!
So what the heck!
Here's what we recommend—
The greatest gift in life's a friend.
Pays a daily dividend.

Be like us and start a trend—
Be friends to the end!"

© "Friends to the End"

"A cat and a mouse? Friends?" said Tom. "No way!"

"That goes double for me!" said Jerry, shaking his tiny head.

"Well, you can't say we didn't warn you," Puggsy said, as he and Frankie left the alley.

"Where'd they go?" asked Tom, scratching his head.

Jerry shrugged.

CLANK! SLAM! SLAM! SLAM!

Tom peeked around the corner in time to see a dogcatcher's van driving away with Puggsy and Frankie locked in back. Suddenly the alley seemed very dark and empty.

"What's out there, pal?" Jerry asked, as he looked into the shadows.

"Quiet, mouse," Tom said, "and *don't* call me pal. Just follow me."

OUT AND ALONE IN THE COLD, CRUEL WORLD

As it got darker and darker, Tom and Jerry got hungrier and hungrier. After wandering for hours, they came to the edge of town. A rushing sound told them they were close to the river.

When they reached the bank, a small figure darted through the shadows. "Who … who are you?" said a high, trembling voice from the darkness.

"He's Tom, and I'm Jerry."

A little girl carrying a backpack stepped out of the darkness. "I thought you were some-body else and you were following me."

"Heck, no!" said Tom. "We're just lost and homeless."

"I'm Robyn Starling—and *I* don't have a home either. Mother died when I was a baby."

"What about your father?" asked Jerry.

Robyn opened a gold locket and showed them the pictures inside. "Daddy was climbing a mountain when the snow gave way in an avalanche." Robyn sobbed, "He was the most wonderful father in the world! We had our own secret place called Robyn's Nest."

"Are you going there now?" Jerry asked.

"Uh-huh," said Robyn. "To get away from my mean Aunt Figg. She's not *really* my aunt—but she and her dog, Ferdinand, took over the house since Daddy's been gone. I'm *never* going back. Aunt Figg acts sweet, but under-neath she's real mean!"

"Ah, c'mon," Tom said kindly. "I'll bet she's crying her eyes out this minute!"

"My poor little Robyn!" Aunt Figg wailed. "Find her, Officer, please! I don't know how I'll live without her!"

"Don't worry. I'll find your niece, lady." The officer left the mansion.

"You *won't* be able to live without her, Pristine." Lickboot, the family lawyer, sank into a plush sofa.

"Shut up, Lickboot, you numbskull!" snapped Aunt Figg, back to her nasty self.

"But it's true, Pristine," said Lickboot. "Without Robyn, Daddy Starling's mansion and the billions of dollars will go bye-bye-bye and you'll be out in the cold, cold, cold."

"And so will *you,* Lickboot," Aunt Figg snarled. "Now stop talking and think! *You're* the lawyer!"

"Hee-hee-hee," Ferdinand, the overfed dachshund, sniggered from under the table.

"Shut up, Ferdy, you fat freeloader!" said Aunt Figg.

"Just pray that the police find her, Pristine," Lickboot said seriously. "Otherwise, we'll be poor for the rest of our lives."

Aunt Figg gasped. "We've got to have money!"

Swept away by the very thought of money, Aunt Figg and Lickboot broke into song:

Money is such a beautiful word!
It soars in my mind like a beautiful bird.
Better than that,
It makes me feel like an aristocrat.
That's where it's at.
Money is such a beautiful word!

Money is such a wonderful thing,
I find that I use it for everything!
Money is power.
If it were food, it's a dish I'd devour,
Every hour.
Money is such a beautiful word!

Money's my passion,
Always in fashion.
Stashin' cash,
Creaming the cream,
That is my dream!

Money's my favorite,
That's why I crave it.
Bein' a rich,
Wicked old witch,
Why should I switch!

Money's the love of my life.
The only true love of my life.

Money and I,
We are as happy as apple an' pie.
Haven't you heard?
Money is such a beautiful word!

Money, they say, is as evil as Satan,
And probably worse.
A dreadful and wonderful curse.
A pleasure to have in my purse!
Money is the most beautiful word!!

© "Money is Such a Beautiful Word"

DING-DONG! The doorbell rang at the Starling mansion.

Aunt Figg rushed to the door and opened it to find the police officer with Robyn in hand, struggling to break free. "I can't go back!"

Aunt Figg cackled with greedy delight. "We got you back, you little—" Then she remembered the officer. "You little dar-ling!"

"We found her down by the bridge, ma'am." The police officer tightened his grip.

Just then, Tom and Jerry appeared in the doorway. They had chased the patrol car all the way back to the mansion.

"Tom! Jerry!" Robyn called happily.

"Whoooo?" Aunt Figg oozed, glaring at the cat and mouse.

Robyn broke free from the officer's grip and hugged her new friends. "This is Tom, and this is Jerry," she said to her aunt. "Can I keep them? They won't bother you. Pleeeease?"

"It might be good for her to have pets," said the officer as he headed toward his car.

"That's just what I was thinking," Aunt Figg lied. "Of course you can keep them—dar-ling."

"I *can?*" said Robyn.

"Ferdy, show our guests to the kitchen, and give them something special to eat," ordered Aunt Figg. As Ferdinand rolled toward the kitchen on his skateboard, with Tom and Jerry at his tail, Aunt Figg grabbed Robyn. "As for you, *orphan,* you're going to bed without dinner."

After eating, Tom and Jerry climbed a grand staircase to look for Robyn. At the top, Jerry noticed a mouse hole and poked his head in to explore. It was empty. He crept inside and found himself in a narrow tunnel, with a light at the other end. Too curious to turn back now, he scurried toward the light and found himself staring down into a room with tall bookcases. In fact, he was on a bookcase himself, peering right down at Aunt Figg. Jerry crouched behind a brass fish statuette just as Lickboot rushed in with a telegram.

"Pristine," he cried, Robyn's father is alive! He was found lying on a mountainside in Tibet."

"Alive?" Aunt Figg didn't want to believe what she was hearing. "Daddy Starling is *alive?*"

"This telegram says he survived the avalanche."

"*ALIVE!*" yelled Aunt Figg. "Does anybody *else* know about this?"

Lickboot shook his head and gave her a sly look. "Just you and me."

"Then it'll be our secret. Robyn must never know." Aunt Figg crumpled up the telegram and tossed it into the fireplace. "I'll lock her in the attic."

Lickboot leered back at her, "That's the best idea I've heard all day." And they left the room, closing the big oak doors behind them.

As soon as they were gone, Jerry scrambled down the bookcase, grabbed the telegram from the fireplace, stomped out the flames, and rushed back up the bookcase again. He raced back through the tunnel, and bumped **SMACK!** into Tom.

"Hold it, mousie. What's the big rush?" asked Tom.

Jerry tried to catch his breath. "Robyn's father is still alive!" He showed Tom the telegram. "We have to tell Robyn!"

"How nice!" Aunt Figg's voice cut through the air above them.

Tom and Jerry froze. Aunt Figg snatched the telegram from Tom and grabbed him by the tail. "I'm afraid you two can't stay *here* any longer. I'll see to it that Dr. Applecheek takes *special* care of you."

"Har-har-har," Ferdinand chuckled from his skateboard perch under the table.

Aunt Figg threw Tom and Jerry into a pet carrier and put it into her car. After a short drive, Aunt Figg pulled up in front of a cheery white house with pink shutters and a garden. Tom and Jerry looked at each other in surprise. Not bad!

The door was opened by a smiling man with rosy cheeks. "Dr. J. Sweetface Applecheek, at your service, my dear lady."

"Miss Pristine Figg, Doctor." Aunt Figg handed him the pet carrier. "Here are two sweet strays my darling little niece brought home. We don't have any room for them, but I was told you do."

"Certainly," said Dr. Applecheek. "My loving home is a shelter for all our lost and abandoned animal friends.

They'll be in good hands." As Aunt Figg left, he smiled and closed the door.

"Now, cat and mouse, I'll give you a tour of your new home." Dr. Applecheek opened a door leading to the basement. "Here, boys! Take good care of them!" Breaking into a fit of fiendish laughter, Dr. Applecheek tossed Tom and Jerry down the stairs into the damp darkness.

CLANK! They were locked in.

"We have to get out of here," Tom whispered.

"But how?" Jerry whispered back.

"See those buttons?" said a gruff voice from the next cage. "Somebody's got to get over there and press them."

"I think *I* can do it," said Jerry. With that, he squeezed through the bars, scurried across the floor, climbed up the control panel, and jumped from one button to the next, unlocking all the cages.

"Everybody out," Tom whispered.

Seconds later, the basement was filled with dogs, cats, and other animals following Tom toward the stairs. Jerry rode on Tom's shoulder.

"Quiet down there!" yelled Dr. Applecheek, when he heard the commotion—but it was too late. **WHACK!** He was trampled by Tom and the others. Free at last!

NOW TO FIND ROBYN AND TELL HER THE NEWS!

WOULD ROBYN EVER SEE HER FATHER AGAIN?

*D*o I miss you?
Count the stars,
Multiply by ten,
'Course I do …
More than now and then.

I could paint a rainbow,
Shine the sky,
Set the stars in space,
Faster than explain
How much I miss your face.

Watch the moon,
Someday soon
He will start to smile
When I say
I'll see you in a while.

But till then I'll miss you,
Dry my tears.
Hide my fears away
Until that happy day.
To the rainbow's end
Is where I would go, my friend,
I do miss you so.

© "I Miss You"

TAP. TAP. TAP. The sound brought Robyn back to her senses.

"Jerry! Tom!" she cried, opening the window as she recognized her two friends.

"Robyn, have we got news for you!" Jerry dropped onto the sill.

"Your father's alive," said Tom, climbing in after him.

Robyn gasped. "Daddy's alive!"

Tom and Jerry nodded and grinned excitedly at Robyn.

"I've got to go find him," Robyn declared. I'm sure he needs me." She opened a dresser drawer, and began to yank out clothes. "I'd better dress warm. It'll be cold in Tibet!"

"Tibet!" Tom and Jerry couldn't believe their ears.

"If that's where my daddy is, *that's* where I'm going!" Robyn said.

"Do you have any idea where Tibet is?" asked Tom.

"Uh … not exactly. Do you?"

"It's way-way-way …" Jerry began.

"Past Cleveland," finished Tom. He was just guessing.

But nothing could stop Robyn. She made a rope of bed sheets and lowered it out the window. Tom and Jerry looked at each other. They knew they couldn't let Robyn go alone. The three of them climbed down, trying to be as quiet as possible.

"What's that noise?"

Once on the ground, they were not sure which way to go. "I think the river is that way!" Tom panted, and led the way to the water.

"What's that ... over there?" Robyn paused and tried to catch her breath.

"It's just an old crate," Tom said, disappointed.

Jerry hopped aboard. "Wrong again, Tom! It's a raft!" He even found a wooden oar.

The three of them began to push the crate toward the river, but suddenly they froze at the sight of headlights! **CLICK. SLAM. CLICK. SLAM.** Three shadows—they could tell one was a dog—got out of a car.

"Shhhh, it's Aunt Figg."

In a sugar-sweet voice, Aunt Figg cried, "Yoo-hoo! Robyn Starling! It's your Auntie Figg, dar-ling. I've come to take you home!"

"Hurry, get on the raft," Robyn whispered. Tom leapt onto the raft, and Jerry followed, but **SPLASH!** didn't make it. Tom reached into the water and pulled him onto the raft by his tiny ears. They shoved off the bank and started floating downstream.

"Whacka-whacka-wow!" yapped Ferdinand, trying to alert Aunt Figg. "We should have left you home," she snapped at him.

Ferdinand tried again. "Rr-Robyn-rruff!" "Oh, shut up!" Annoyed, and still ignoring him, Aunt Figg gave Ferdinand a kick.

He tumbled backward off the bridge, slipped down the slope, and plopped into the water. "Arf … watch out … arr!" he grunted as he started to sink.

Ferdinand tried to dog-paddle to the raft, but he was too fat to catch up with Robyn and her pals. Instead, he sank lower into the water.

Swiftly carrying Robyn, Tom, and Jerry away from their pursuers, the raft bobbed gently on the open water. Soon they were all asleep. After a while, an odd sound roused Tom.

Pocketa-pocketa-pocketa.

Tom was so startled he fell off the raft.

Pocketa-pocKETA-POCKETA.

Robyn opened her eyes. A giant steamer loomed out of the fog—heading straight toward them.

POCKETA-POCKETA-POCKETA!

"Yeow!" screeched Tom.

"Huh?" said Jerry, rubbing his sleepy eyes.

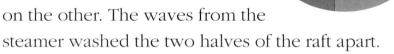

SMASH! CRASH! The ship sliced the raft in two, with Tom and Jerry on one half and Robyn on the other. The waves from the steamer washed the two halves of the raft apart.

POCKETA-POCKeta-pocketa. The ship faded out of sight.

Meanwhile, above the Himalaya Mountains, all the way across the world, Daddy Starling was flying his plane through a terrible storm. Someone was trying to reach him over the radio, but there was so much static, it was hard to hear.

"What? My daughter's run away!" he shouted after hearing the message. Before the voice could answer him, the radio went dead.

Daddy Starling pulled off his headset. "If Robyn's in trouble, there's only one place she'll go." He turned the plane around and headed for Robyn's Nest.

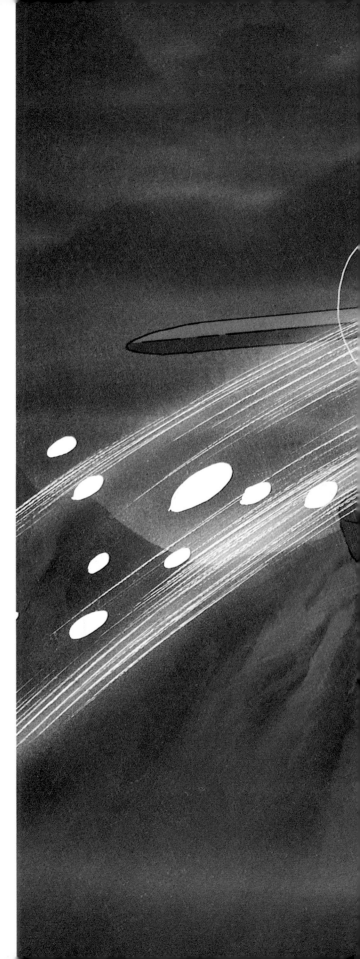

Back at the mansion, Aunt Figg was horrified. "No more *money?*" she screamed.

"That's right, Pristine," Lickboot said. "There's only one way we can get Daddy Starling's money. We just have to prove that we're taking care of Robyn. But we can't prove it since Robyn's not here."

"I *know* Robyn's not here, you nerdy nitwit," screeched Aunt Figg. "I'm counting on *you* to lie, cheat, steal—*any*thing to get her back here!"

"How about offering a reward?" Lickboot said.

"Yes, a reward!" Aunt Figg raised an eyebrow.

Lickboot rushed out to his car and brought back a milk carton. "Like this?" he said, holding up the carton. On the carton was a picture of Robyn and a notice offering a million-dollar reward.

"Good work, Lickboot." Aunt Figg evilly grinned her approval. "Good, sleazy work."

"Heh-heh-heh," Ferdy chuckled to himself in his corner.

"*This* will get the little brat back." Aunt Figg laughed until the whole mansion shook.

A FEW MILES DOWN THE RIVER WAS A CARNIVAL....

2310

"Great wobbling wattles!" said Captain Kiddie. He couldn't believe his eyes. A little girl clinging to a piece of wood had drifted onto his beach.

"Aaaaaaawk! Let's bring her home," his parrot suggested.

The captain carried the small girl to his trailer and tucked her into bed, where she slept for three days and three nights. On the fourth morning she began to stir....

"Aaaaaah!" Robyn screamed, when she saw the parrot staring at her.

"Sorry, my dear," the captain apologized. "My first mate doesn't always mind his manners."

"It's me bad upbringing to blame," squawked the parrot.

"Don't pay attention to him," said the man. "You are the lucky guest of me—Captain Kiddie, King of the County Fair, Pirate of Pleasure—"

"Aaaaaaawk!"

"Oh, yes ... and this here is my first mate, Squawk."

"He's funny," Robyn giggled. She began to feel a bit more comfortable around these two.

"You must be hungry," Captain Kiddie said. "You've been lying here for a few days now."

"Really?" Robyn felt dizzy. "I'm starving!" she said.

"I'll bet you'd like some milk and cookies. And milk and cookies is just what we got."

"It's *all* we got," muttered Squawk.

"So, where'd you say you were headed, little lady?" Captain Kiddie asked Robyn as she ate her cookies.

"Tibet."

"Tibet?" Captain Kiddie scratched his head. "I know Tibet real well. Why, it's just outside of Cleveland, right?" He poured her a glass of milk.

"Aaawk! Aaawk!" Squawk fluttered nervously around the milk carton.

"What is it?" Captain Kiddie said angrily. Then he noticed the picture on the milk carton. It was a picture of the same little girl who sat next to him. And someone was offering a million-dollar reward for her! Captain Kiddie and Squawk excused themselves and went outside.

"I'm rich! I'm rich!" Captain Kiddie yelled gleefully.

"You mean _we're_ rich!" Squawk corrected him.

"Oh, yeah, I forgot," said Captain Kiddie. "We've hit the jackpot!"

BRRRINNG! BRRRINNG! Aunt Figg's telephone rang.

"Hello?"

"Hmmmm, Miss Pristine Figg?"

"Who is this?"

"What a lovely name you have. It sounds like a million dollars."

"Who is this, and what do you want?"

"Captain Kiddie here, and I'm calling to claim my reward. Your little girl is safe with me at the one and only Captain Kiddie's Carnival."

"My precious little Robyn? At Captain Kiddie's Carnival!"

Aunt Figg slammed down the phone. "Come on, Ferdy, Lickboot—get in the car. We've got her!"

"No, *I've* got her!" said a voice from the front porch. It was Applecheek, who had overheard everything.

Applecheek had no time to lose. Aunt Figg, Lickboot, and Ferdy were already speeding away in Lickboot's red convertible. If he reached the fairgrounds before them, he could kidnap Robyn and claim the reward for himself. But he didn't have a car. Looking around, he grabbed the first vehicle he could find—an ice-cream truck. It was better than nothing!

Meanwhile, Tom and Jerry drifted slowly down the river on what was left of the wooden raft. Jerry watched fish flip-flopping in and out of the water as Tom slept soundly at his side. Tom's rumbling belly gave Jerry an idea.

He'd go fishing! Tom could wake up to fresh fish for breakfast. It was nice being friends for a change—sort of. Of course, Tom kept reminding him that he was boss, but things were going just fine. Jerry tiptoed over to Tom and carefully dipped the tip of his tail in the water as if it were a fishing line. And sure enough, a fish swam over to the tail and—

"Yeeeeooooow!" Tom jumped ten feet in the air. The fish had bitten his tail and was still hanging on!

"Oops," Jerry whispered, prying the fish's jaws off of Tom's tail.

"What are you doing, mouse!"

"Catching your breakfast." Jerry blushed innocently.

"Okay, mousie. You wanna *really* catch something?" Without waiting for an answer, he picked up Jerry and prepared to fling him far out into the water when—

THUD!

They had washed ashore.

"Hey, look at that." Tom pointed toward a sparkle in a thatch of bushes.

Jerry rushed over to the bushes and lifted up a beautiful necklace. "It's Robyn's locket!" he cried.

Tom bent over and picked up the locket. "She *must* be around here somewhere," he said.

"Hey, look over there, Tom."

Tom turned to see a carnival off in the distance.

"How 'bout a ride on the captain's Ferris wheel?" Captain Kiddie led Robyn to the base. "It's the tallest one in the county."

"Aaawk! It's the *only* one in the county," Squawk added.

"You get a great view from the top," Captain Kiddie bragged.

"I … uh … love Ferris wheels," Robyn said, "but I don't … uh … think this one looks too sturdy." But Captain Kiddie had already strapped her into the seat.

"You'll love this one, little girl." Captain Kiddie pulled the START lever. "It's very safe."

"Yeah," Squawk said. "We wouldn't want anything to happen to Robyn Starling."

Robyn stared at him. "Uh … wait. How'd you know my name?"

But it was too late. With a shudder and a creak, the car began to rise.

"Sorry, kid. Gotta keep you here till your aunt comes to fetch you," Captain Kiddie said.

Tears filled Robyn's eyes. "And I thought you were a nice man."

"But I am, dear." Captain Kiddie looked hurt.

"Aaawk. But he'll be even nicer with a million smackeroos."

"Don't send me back to Aunt Figg," Robyn pleaded. "She hates me."

Captain Kiddie pulled the lever to STOP just as Robyn reached the top. The car jolted, and Robyn accidentally let go of the balloon she was holding. She looked after the balloon sadly as it floated away.

"Nap time for the old captain," Kiddie said, and settled himself into a chair.

Robyn was terrified! She was higher than the treetops! Suddenly another balloon floated toward her. A bit startled, she reached out for the string and the car began to sway. Holding onto the side, she grabbed the string—and attached to the end of it was her gold locket!

"My locket!" Keeping both hands on the car, she looked over the edge. Everything looked miniature—the rides, the people, and—"Tom! Jerry!"

Her two friends were on the ground looking up at her. Tom signaled for her to be quiet so as not to wake Captain Kiddie. They sneaked over to the lever—but it wouldn't budge.

Tom and Jerry struggled and struggled until finally the lever moved to START.

"Tom, it's moving!" Robyn called with excitement. Down, down, down she went until she reached the bottom. Then Tom cranked the lever to STOP. Robyn climbed out of the seat and went to hug her friends.

"Uh-oh," Jerry said, peering over Robyn's shoulder. "Don't look now, but here comes the dragon lady."

SCREECH. SLAM. SLAM. Aunt Figg, Lickboot, and Ferdinand had arrived.

"Where's the girl?" Aunt Figg demanded, shaking the captain awake. Luckily, Tom and Jerry were hidden from her view.

"Aargh … What the …!" Captain Kiddie rubbed his eyes.

Squawk looked Aunt Figg up and down. "We wants to see the money, honey."

"Only *after* I see my precious Robyn," Aunt Figg snapped.

"There she is!" Lickboot pointed to Robyn as she got out of the Ferris wheel car.

"Yah-yah-yah," Ferdinand sniggered.

"The million-dollar kid!" Captain Kiddie shouted happily.

"Oh, Robyn, sweetie, come to your dear Aunt Figgie," Aunt Figg called. "Don't let the brat get by you!" she hissed under her breath to Lickboot and Ferdinand.

Tom, Jerry, and Robyn looked around in a panic. "What'll we do now?" Robyn asked.

"I'll get us outta here. Come on!" Tom led them to a paddleboat that belonged to Captain Kiddie. Quickly, they hopped aboard.

"Don't we need keys?" Robyn asked.

"Not if we can help it." Jerry leapt onto a red button while Tom slammed back the accelerator.

It worked! The twin paddle wheels started to move, spraying Aunt Figg and the others who stood on the pier. The boat lurched forward and headed toward deeper water.

THE THREE FRIENDS MADE A RUN FOR IT!

CAPTAIN KIDDIE'S RAFT ZIPPED OVER THE WATER...

"Aye! Move it, Cap'n. Move it!" Squawk screeched. "We're in a race for a million dollars!"

"Not to worry, mate. This old captain still knows a trick or two." Captain Kiddie climbed into a small rubber raft and cranked up the out-board motor. Squawk flapped his wings excitedly as the raft sped out toward the paddleboat.

"Let me steer! Let me steer!" squawked Squawk.

"Out of the way, birdbrain. *I'm* captain here!"

"They're getting away!"
screeched Aunt Figg. "Lickboot!
Do something!"

"What can *I* do now? I'm just
a lawyer."

"You're just an idiot!" Aunt
Figg growled. "Get in the car and
we'll catch that brat and her friends
up the river. They'll have to come
to shore eventually. They'll need
to eat...."

"They can catch fish," Lickboot
suggested, pulling into the road.
"That's what I would do."

"Oh, shut up, you no-good
lawyer." Aunt Figg snarled.

"Heh-heh-heh!" Ferdy sniggered.

"You, too, fat slob!" Aunt Figg
yelled. "And, Lickboot,
drive
faster!"

FERDIE HIT THE BOARDS!

SCCRREEEECHH!
Lickboot swung the car around and pressed the gas pedal as far as it would go. Finally, he lost control, skidded, and plowed straight through a fence. Ferdinand flew out of the car.

"Aaargh! Wait for me!" Ferdinand rolled after the car at full speed.

But Aunt Figg and Lickboot wouldn't stop for anything. They were gaining on the paddleboat, which was speeding through the water, with Tom steering and Robyn and Jerry keeping an eye on Aunt Figg's car. "Faster, Tom!"

"They're getting away!" Lickboot put both feet on the gas pedal.

SCCCREEEECHH! The car's wheels churned forward, spraying mud in Ferdinand's face while the dog hung on for dear life.

They passed Applecheek, who was chugging along in the ice-cream truck. He'd never reach Robyn before Aunt Figg did. Neither would Captain Kiddie and Squawk. They were too busy arguing.

"Let go of the wheel, I tell you. *I'm* the captain, and *I'll* do the steering!" Captain Kiddie demanded.

Squawk held on tight. "You couldn't steer your way around a bathtub."

Lickboot drove across a rickety bridge, dragging Ferdinand behind. Ferdinand bounced into the air, then plunged headlong through the rotting planks into the river. **"OOH! UMPH! OW!"**

When Applecheek reached the bridge, it was too late—"Aahhhh!" He broke through the planks and fell onto Captain Kiddie's raft.

"Aaaawwwk!" They were out of the race.

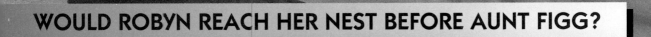

WOULD ROBYN REACH HER NEST BEFORE AUNT FIGG?

"Well, that takes care of Captain Kiddie and Applecheek," said Tom. Robyn and Jerry giggled.

"But what happened to Aunt Figg?" Jerry looked puzzled.

Tom shrugged. "I think we lost them, mouse. What do you think, Robyn?"

But Robyn wasn't paying attention. She was too busy looking at the shoreline. "This place looks familiar," she said.

"What do you mean, Robyn?" Jerry asked.

"*Yes!*" Robyn jumped up. "I know where we are. We're headed straight for Robyn's Nest. You know—that special place I told you about. Just mine and my daddy's." Tom steered the paddleboat toward shore.

Lickboot reached a sign for Robyn's Nest.

"Turn!" Aunt Figg demanded. The red convertible swerved onto the road. They were sure to arrive before Robyn, Tom, and Jerry. This was the shortcut!

"Here it is! This is the cabin!" Excitedly, Robyn raced up the stone steps that led to the small wooden cabin. Tom and Jerry followed. "Daddy built this place just for me. We'd come up here to swim and sail and fish and … Daddy will know where to find me. Maybe he's here already."

But the place looked deserted.

"I hope Robyn won't be too disappointed if her father isn't here." Jerry whispered.

"I know what you mean." Tom was worried.

Robyn flung open the door. The cabin was dark. "Daddy? Daddy? Dad-dy?"

Suddenly a lantern flared up and cast an evil glow on Aunt Figg's face. "Daddy is dead!" she shouted.

"Aaaaaaahhhhh!" Robyn screamed as loud as she could. "Tom! Jerry! Help!" But it was too late. Lickboot had slammed and locked the door behind her. Tom and Jerry were left outside.

"You're *not* taking me back," Robyn said, gritting her teeth.

Lickboot grabbed her arm. "Oh, yes we are."

"Don't touch me!" Robyn kicked Lickboot in the left shin.

"Way to go, Robyn!" Tom and Jerry watched through the window.

"Ow! Ow! Ow!" Lickboot hopped up and down on his right leg. He fell backward, knocking over the lantern. Its flame spread quickly to the rug—and then the curtains. Seconds later, the whole room was ablaze with bright orange flames.

"You fools!" shouted Aunt Figg. "Lickboot, grab the girl and let's get out of here."

But Robyn was too quick for them and made a dash for the stairs. Lickboot started to follow her.

"Lickboot!" shouted Aunt Figg. "The cabin is burning down! Let's get out of here before we all fry!"

"But the girl—"

"Forget her, Lickboot!" Aunt Figg screamed. "We've got to save *ourselves!*" Smoke was beginning to curl around the edges of the front door.

Unable to find the key to the locked door, Lickboot and Figg tried to break through it. Ferdinand, who had by this time recovered from his dousing in the river, was resting by the door. As Lickboot crashed through it, he slipped on Ferdinand's

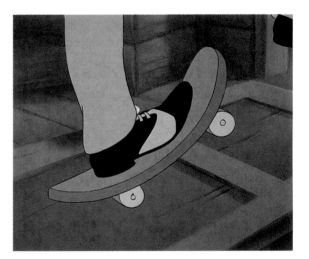

skateboard, flipping Ferdinand into the air and sending Aunt Figg flying forward.

Bumpity-bumpity-BUMP! They slid down the steps of the wooden pier toward the river.

The trio slipped, flipped, and went flying! Aunt Figg and Lickboot landed in the crow's nest of Captain Kiddie's paddleboat. Ferdy fell on the throttle, which accidentally started the engine. The paddles began to turn around and around, and the boat headed out onto the river, wobbling from side to side.

Lickboot, you oaf! OOF!

82

"She's going upstairs!" Tom plucked Jerry away from the window, grabbed a rope from the porch, and made a dash for a drainpipe that led to the roof. When they reached the roof, Tom pried open a skylight.

"Robyn! Are you down there?" Tom called.

"Tom! Jerry!" Robyn's voice was weak and frightened, but at least they could hear her. "The cabin is burning and ..."

"Grab hold of the knot." Tom lowered the rope through the skylight.

"And don't be scared," Jerry added.

Robyn climbed the rope, while the flames grew higher and hotter, barely missing her as they broke through the walls. Tom and Jerry helped her crawl onto the roof to safety.

But safe, they weren't. Flames came from all directions. "How will we get off the roof?" Robyn asked desperately.

Tom and Jerry looked at each other blankly. What could they do now?

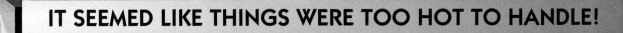

IT SEEMED LIKE THINGS WERE TOO HOT TO HANDLE!

Just then, they heard a loud thundering sound. They looked up to see a helicopter approaching!

"Look!" Tom and Jerry shouted. "Someone's coming to save us!"

Robyn looked where they were pointing. "Daddy! Daddy! Daddy!" She waved her arms in all directions.

"Robyn, darling," Daddy Starling called. "I'm coming! Hang on to the roof!"

As the helicopter came closer, it got windier and windier. A flurry of bright embers and smoke swirled around Robyn, Tom, and Jerry. Soon the helicopter was hovering in the air, next to the roof. Robyn's father reached out for her. "Take my hand, sweetheart! Hurry!"

Robyn struggled against the wind. She reached up … and lost her balance! But Daddy Starling grabbed her just in time and scooped her up into the helicopter.

Suddenly a gust of wind sent pieces of the roof flying into the river. **CRA-AACK.** The roof was caving in! A burst of flames shot up around Tom and Jerry. Scared for their lives, they looked into each other's eyes. What could they do now? They were doomed!

"Tom! Jer-ry!" Robyn's voice was getting farther and farther away. Another gust of wind came up and more parts of the roof flew into the water. A shower of steam and sparks rose from the river.

"Hold on, Jerry!" Tom screamed.

"I can't!"

Tom reached out for Jerry, but it was too late. The whole roof gave way to the flames, and Tom and Jerry fell down ... down ... down ... disappearing into the midst of smoke and flame as the cabin crashed into the river.

The water was littered with burnt rafters, shingles, and other wreckage from the cabin, which was now just a pile of ashes.

Suddenly Tom poked his head out of the water. Gasping for air, he began searching for Jerry. "Jerry! Jerry, where are you? Oh, don't leave me, little buddy. What would I *do* without you?" He gulped. "You were the best pal a guy could ever have. Oh, please be alive. I promise you…"

"All the cheese I can eat?" said Jerry, who, at that moment, was floating behind Tom in a chipped soap dish.

"I promise you all the cheese you can eat," Tom continued, "and—"

"No more traps?" said Jerry.

"No more traps," said Tom.

"And no tricks?"

"And no tricks."

"That's a promise?"

"That's a … hey, wait a minute!" Tom whirled around and glared at Jerry. "Ooh … I'm gonna … Why you little …"

At last, the helicopter landed in a clearing near the water, and Daddy Starling helped Robyn out. Robyn's eyes were red from crying. "I can't bear the thought of never seeing Tom or Jerry again."

"Tom and Jerry wouldn't want to see you sad." Daddy Starling tried to comfort his daughter.

"But I can't help it. If it wasn't for them, we'd never have found each other. We took a boat down the river—" Robyn looked out at the water and her face broke into a great big smile.

"Tom! Jerry! You're safe!" She ran toward them. Her father followed.

"Daddy," said Robyn, "I want you to meet my two best friends, Tom and Jerry—the ones I was telling you about."

Her father smiled at Jerry and patted Tom on the head. "I want to thank you for helping my daughter," he said. "I promise never to leave her again."

"Oh, Daddy!" Robyn said happily. She picked up Jerry and set him on her father's shoulder. And the four of them huddled together in a big bear hug.

A WEEK LATER AT THE STARLING MANSION...

Tom stretched lazily. Afternoon naps were great! His new bed was much more comfortable than his old one. Bigger and better. Everything was better—especially the fresh cream for breakfast. This was the life!

PIT-PAT. PIT-PAT.

Tom opened one eye and saw Jerry heading toward his new mouse hole with a huge hunk of cheese. Jerry waved.

Tom waved back. This life was agreeing with Jerry, too. He sure looked good. He seemed well-rested. And well-fed. And fat. And ... hmmm. Tom grinned mischievously. He could hear Robyn and Daddy Starling in the kitchen baking cookies. The coast was clear! Quietly, Tom crept up to Jerry's doorway.

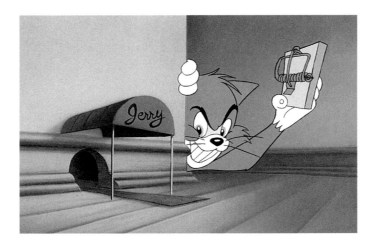

Now all he had to do was wait....